W9-BUC-600

REBEL'S REPORT

ROGUE ONE: VOLUME 6

OPERATIVES:

Jyn Erso and Rebel Intelligence officer Cassian Andor have disobeyed direct orders and assembled a ragtag group of rebel fighters to infiltrate the Imperial base on Scarif.

JYN ERSO

CAPTAIN CASSIAN ANDOR

MISSION:

Launch a rebel incursion in order to steal the Death Star plans and reveal the strategic weakness within the weapon, placed there by Imperial scientist and father of Jyn Erso, Galen Erso (deceased).

GALEN ERSO

NOTES:

Imperial Director Krennic, having discovered Galen Erso's treason, has arrived on Scarif to investigate the security leak.

ORSON KRENNIC

CREDITS:

WRITER • Jody Houser
ARTIST • Emilio Laiso
COLORIST • Rachelle Rosenberg
LETTERER • VC's Clayton Cowles
COVER ARTIST • Phil Noto
PRODUCTION DESIGN • Carlos Lao
EDITOR • Heather Antos
SUPERVISING EDITOR • Jordan D. White
EXECUTIVE EDITOR • C.B. Cebulski
EDITOR IN CHIEF • Axel Alonso
CHIEF CREATIVE OFFICER • Joe Quesada
PRESIDENT • Dan Buckley
EXECUTIVE PRODUCER • Alan Fine

Based on the screenplay by Chris Weitz and Tony Gilroy
Based on a story by John Knoll and Gary Whitta

LUCASFILM:

SENIOR EDITOR • Frank Parisi
CREATIVE DIRECTOR • Michael Siglain
LUCASFILM STORY GROUP • James Waugh, Leland Chee, Matt Martin, Rayne Roberts

ABDOPUBLISHING.COM

Reinforced library bound edition published in 2019 by Spotlight,
a division of ABDO, PO Box 398166, Minneapolis, Minnesota 55439.
Spotlight produces high-quality reinforced library bound editions for
schools and libraries. Published by agreement with Marvel Characters, Inc.

Printed in the United States of America, North Mankato, Minnesota.
042018
092018

Library of Congress Control Number: 2017961400

Publisher's Cataloging in Publication Data

Names: Houser, Jody, author. | Laiso, Emilio; Bazaldua, Oscar; Rosenberg, Rachelle; Villanelli, Paolo, illustrators.
Title: Rogue One / writer: Jody Houser; art: Emilio Laiso, Oscar Bazaldua, Rachelle Rosenberg, and Paolo Villanelli.
Description: Reinforced library bound edition. | Minneapolis, MN : Spotlight, 2019 | Series: Star Wars: Rogue One | Volume 1 written by Jody Houser; illustrated by Emilio Laiso, Oscar Bazaldua and Rachelle Rosenberg. | Volumes 2, 4, 5, and 6 written by Jody Houser; illustrated by Emilio Laiso and Rachelle Rosenberg. | Volume 3 written by Jody Houser; illustrated by Paolo Villanelli and Rachelle Rosenberg.
Summary: Scientist Galen Erso is taken from his home and forced to work on the Empire's secret planet-killing weapon, leaving his daughter, Jyn, to grow up on her own. Fifteen years later, Galen leaks information on the weapon, through a message he sends to some bandits on the moon Jedha. Now, the rebels of the Alliance want to know if the rumors of an Imperial Death Star are true. They'll need Jyn to help retrieve the message and, possibly, find her father.
Identifiers: ISBN 9781532141683 (Volume 1) | ISBN 9781532141690 (Volume 2) | ISBN 9781532141706 (Volume 3) | ISBN 9781532141713 (Volume 4) | ISBN 9781532141720 (Volume 5) | ISBN 9781532141737 (Volume 6)
Subjects: LCSH: Star Wars films--Juvenile fiction. | Weapons--Juvenile fiction. | Space colonies--Juvenile fiction. | Imaginary wars and battles--Juvenile fiction. | Comic books, strips, etc.--Juvenile fiction.
Classification: DDC 741.5--dc23

Spotlight

A Division of ABDO
abdopublishing.com

SCARIF.
RED AND GOLD SQUADRONS, ATTACK FORMATIONS. DEFEND THE FLEET!
BLUE SQUADRON, GET TO THE SURFACE BEFORE THEY CLOSE THAT GATE!
THIS IS BLUE LEADER.
I COPY YOU, ADMIRAL RADDUS.
YES!

U-WINGS, REINFORCE THOSE TROOPS ON THE BEACH!
ALL FIGHTERS ON ME! WE HAVE TO SHIELD THEM FROM AIR ATTACK!
I'VE GOT ONE ON MY TAIL!
THIS IS BLUE LEADER, I'M ON HIM.
WE'RE HAVING NO EFFECT ON THAT SHIELD!
THEY'RE ALL OVER ME! I'M TRYING TO LOSE THEM! THIS IS RED FIVE, I NEED HELP!

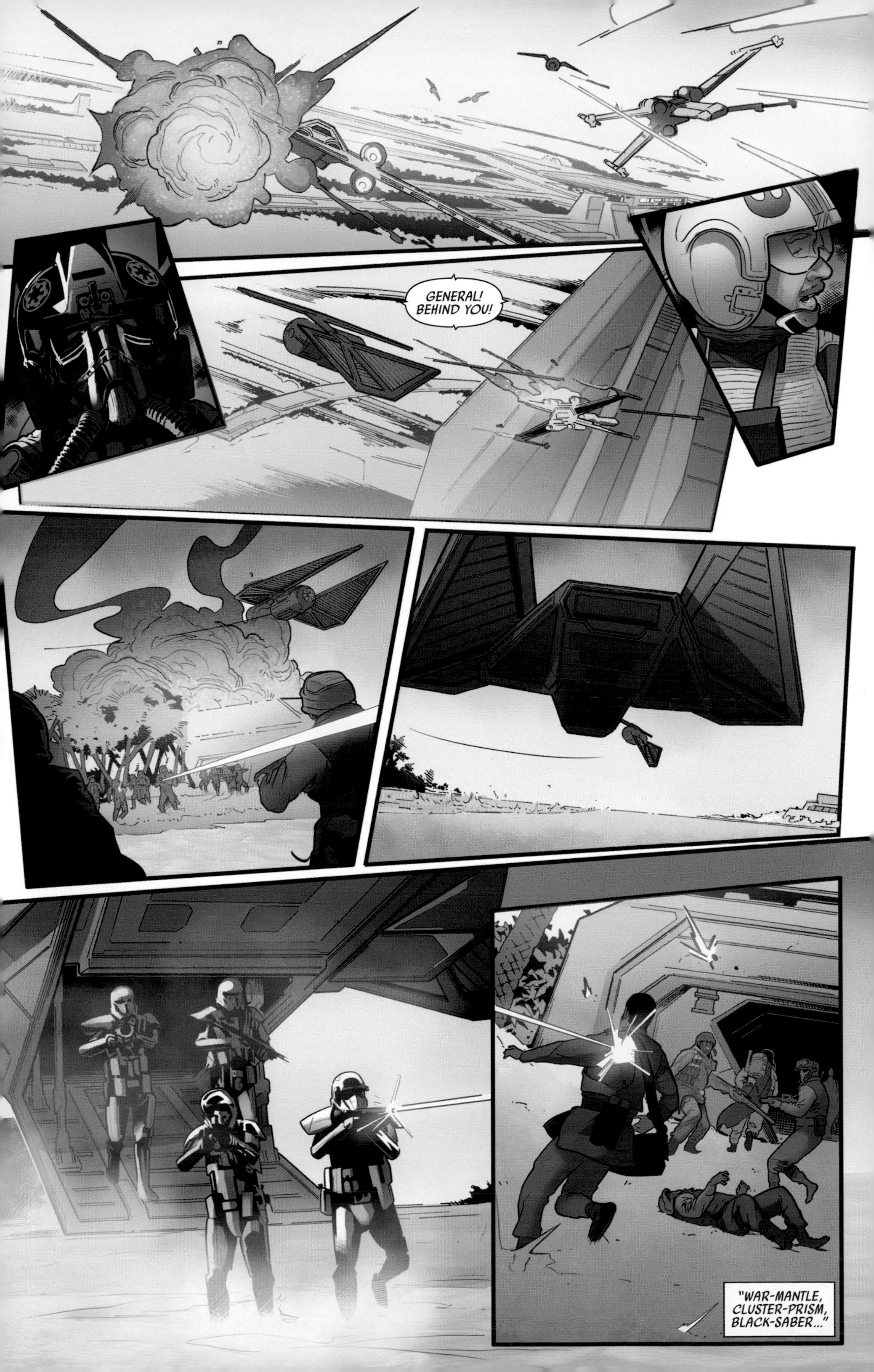
GENERAL! BEHIND YOU!
"WAR-MANTLE, CLUSTER-PRISM, BLACK-SABER..."

STARDUST.
THAT'S IT. THE DEATH STAR PLANS.
HOW DO YOU KNOW THAT?
"I KNOW BECAUSE IT'S ME."
KAYTOO! WE NEED THE FILE FOR STARDUST!
YOU'LL NEED THIS.
YOU WANTED ONE, RIGHT?
YOUR BEHAVIOR, JYN ERSO...
"...IS CONTINUALLY UNEXPECTED."
THAT'S IT.
KAYTOO!

CLIMB! CLIMB!
YOU CAN STILL SEND THE PLANS TO THE FLEET!
IF THEY OPEN THE SHIELD GATE, YOU CAN BROADCAST FROM THE TOWER!
LOCKING THE VAULT DOOR NOW--
GOODBYE.
KAY! KAY!

YOU HAVE TO GET ON THE RADIO, GET MELSHI TO FIND A MASTER SWITCH.
GET HIM TO ACTIVATE THE CONNECTION BETWEEN US AND THAT COMM TOWER.

THEN GO!

"MELSHI, MELSHI, COME IN! ARE YOU THERE?!

"BODHI WILL SEND THE SIGNAL FROM HERE. HE'S PATCHING US IN.

"BUT YOU GUYS HAVE TO OPEN UP A LINE TO THE TOWER..."

WHA-- THE LINE'S SNAGGED!

HEY, YOU!
IDENTIFY YOURSELF!

I'VE GOT IT!
CAREFUL!
UNGH!

I CAN EXPLAI--

BODHI, ARE YOU THERE? DID YOU CALL THE FLEET?!

I CAN'T GET TO THE SHUTTLE! I CAN'T PLUG IN, CASSIAN!
YOU HAVE TO! THEY HAVE TO HIT THAT GATE!
IF THE SHIELD IS OPEN, WE CAN SEND THE PLANS!

MELSHI, MELSHI! COME IN, PLEASE!

I'M TIED IN AT MY END! I JUST NEED AN OPEN LINE!
HANG ON...
THE MASTER SWITCH...
...IT'S OUT THERE, AT THAT CONSOLE...
I'M GOING!
...I AM ONE WITH THE FORCE AND THE FORCE IS WITH ME...
CHIRRUT!

KEEP GOING! KEEP GOING!
CASSIAN!
...I AM ONE WITH THE FORCE AND THE FORCE IS WITH ME...
...I AM ONE WITH THE FORCE AND THE FORCE IS WITH ME...

CHIRRUT, COME! COME WITH ME!
CHIRRUT!
CHIRRUT, DON'T GO. DON'T GO.
I'M HERE. I'M HERE.
IT'S OKAY... IT'S OKAY...
LOOK FOR THE FORCE AND YOU WILL ALWAYS FIND ME...

THAT STAR DESTROYER'S DISABLED!
THIS IS ROGUE ONE, CALLING ANY ALLIANCE SHIPS THAT CAN HEAR ME!
IS THERE ANYBODY UP THERE? THIS IS ROGUE ONE!
COME IN, OVER.
THIS IS ADMIRAL RADDUS ABOARD THE PROFUNDITY! ROGUE ONE, WE HEAR YOU!
THEY FOUND THE DEATH STAR PLANS! THEY HAVE TO TRANSMIT THEM FROM THE COMMUNICATIONS TOWER!
YOU HAVE TO TAKE DOWN THE SHIELD GATE! IT'S THE ONLY WAY TO GET IT THROUGH!
CALL IN A HAMMERHEAD CORVETTE. I HAVE AN IDEA.
STAND BY, ROGUE ONE. WE'RE ON IT.
THIS IS FOR YOU, GALEN...

THE FORCE IS WITH ME...
...AND I AM ONE WITH THE FORCE...
...THE FORCE IS WITH ME...
...AND I AM ONE WITH THE FORCE...
BEEP BEEP BEEP

RESET ANTENNAE ALIGNMENT.
RESET ANTENNAE ALIGNMENT.
RESET ANTENNAE ALIGNMENT.
ANTENNAE ALIGNED. READY TO TRANSMIT.
WHO ARE YOU?

I'M JYN ERSO. DAUGHTER OF GALEN AND LYRA.
YOU'VE LOST.
OH, I HAVE, HAVE I?
SUBLIGHT THRUSTERS! FULL POWER!
MY FATHER'S REVENGE. HE BUILT A FLAW IN THE DEATH STAR.
HE PUT A FUSE IN THE MIDDLE OF YOUR MACHINE AND I'VE JUST TOLD THE ENTIRE GALAXY HOW TO LIGHT IT.
THE SHIELD IS UP. YOUR SIGNAL WILL NEVER REACH THE REBEL BASE.
I'VE LOST NOTHING BUT TIME. YOU, ON THE OTHER HAND, WILL DIE WITH THE REBELLION.

ADMIRAL! RECEIVING TRANSMISSION FROM SCARIF!
WE HAVE THE PLANS!
SHE DID IT...

HEY! LEAVE HIM! LEAVE HIM.

THAT'S IT. THAT'S IT. LET'S GO.

LORD VADER WILL HANDLE THE FLEET. TARGET THE BASE AT SCARIF.
SINGLE REACTOR IGNITION.
"YOU MAY FIRE WHEN READY."
ROGUE ONE... MAY THE FORCE BE WITH YOU.
ALL SHIPS, PREPARE FOR JUMP TO HYPERSPACE!

THE REBEL FLAGSHIP IS DISABLED, LORD VADER.
BUT IT HAS RECEIVED TRANSMISSIONS FROM THE SURFACE.
PREPARE A BOARDING PARTY.
YES, MY LORD.
"YOU THINK ANYBODY'S LISTENING?"
"I DO. SOMEONE'S OUT THERE..."

LAUNCH!

MAKE SURE YOU SECURE THE AIR LOCK. AND PREPARE THE ESCAPE PODS.

YOUR HIGHNESS. THE TRANSMISSION WE RECEIVED.

WHAT IS IT THEY'VE SENT US?

HOPE.

A NEW HOPE

It is a period of civil war. Rebel spaceships, striking from a hidden base, have won their first victory against the evil Galactic Empire.

During the battle, Rebel spies managed to steal secret plans to the Empire's ultimate weapon, the DEATH STAR, an armored space station with enough power to destroy an entire planet.

Pursued by the Empire's sinister agents, Princess Leia races home aboard her starship, custodian of the stolen plans that can save her people and restore freedom to the galaxy....

ROGUE ONE
A STAR WARS STORY

COLLECT THEM ALL!

Set of 6 Hardcover Books ISBN: 978-1-5321-4167-6

ROGUE ONE: VOLUME 1
HOUSER LAISO BAZALDUA ROSENBERG

Hardcover Book ISBN
978-1-5321-4168-3

ROGUE ONE: VOLUME 2
HOUSER LAISO ROSENBERG

Hardcover Book ISBN
978-1-5321-4169-0

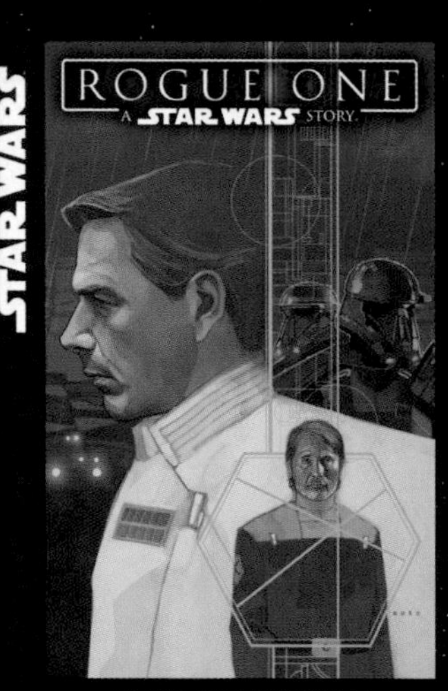

ROGUE ONE: VOLUME 3
HOUSER VILLANELLI ROSENBERG

Hardcover Book ISBN
978-1-5321-4170-6

ROGUE ONE: VOLUME 4
HOUSER LAISO ROSENBERG

Hardcover Book ISBN
978-1-5321-4171-3

ROGUE ONE: VOLUME 5
HOUSER LAISO ROSENBERG

Hardcover Book ISBN
978-1-5321-4172-0

ROGUE ONE: VOLUME 6
HOUSER LAISO ROSENBERG

Hardcover Book ISBN
978-1-5321-4173-7